ESTERHAZY

THE RABBIT PRINCE

STORY BY IRENE DISCHE & HANS MAGNUS ENZENSBERGER

ILLUSTRATED BY MICHAEL SOWA

CREATIVE EDITIONS

Before we begin our story, let us go back a few hundred years, and move over a few hundred miles, to find out how the family Esterhazy got its name.

The very first Esterhazy was originally named Michael Lord Harefoot of Bunnimore, a crowded burrow of London. One night, Lord Harefoot met a young Austrian lady at a ball. He fell in love and married her the next morning. The couple settled down in London, but within a few days, Lady Harefoot began to miss the good Austrian food back home. Soon she was pining away for it: for deep-dish fruit pies, chocolates like tiny treasure chests full of surprises, and cakes with as many layers as a princess's ball gown. Lord Harefoot could not bear to see his new bride unhappy, and so he packed their bags.

After just one rich meal in Austria, he agreed that the food was heavenly. "One does not need to live in London," he said, unpacking their suitcases for good, "to live happily ever after."

The Austrians could not learn to pronounce his name, Harefoot, but he was quite willing to change it. He looked around for a nice name, something splendid but common. He had heard the name *Osterhase* repeated with great respect by Austrians and felt it would do perfectly—not realizing that *Osterhase* actually means "Easter Bunny" in German. However, when Lord Osterhase tried to pronounce his own new name, it came out like this: "Esterhazy." So it turns out that the Esterhazys owe their really very melodious name to Lord Harefoot's poor German. And even that soft "z" in Esterhazy, as amazingly soft as rabbit's fur, was never a handicap for finding a husband or a wife. As we shall now see.

For all sorts of reasons, families tend to have children, and the Esterhazys were no exception. Over the years, the Esterhazys became the largest family in all of Austria. However, none of them were very big. With each generation, the Esterhazys had become smaller and smaller. Probably that was because they preferred eating chocolates and cakes, toffees and pies, to fresh vegetables. By the time our story begins, all the Esterhazys were very, very tiny but very, very intelligent.

Old Lord Esterhazy, still the head of the family, was terribly concerned about the size of his children and grandchildren. They were often laughed right out of shoe stores because even baby shoes were too big. And bicycle riding was impossible since their feet couldn't reach the pedals of the tiniest models. After the smallest Esterhazy fell into a wastepaper basket and couldn't climb back out, Lord Esterhazy said, "This is a disaster. Something must be done."

He locked himself in his room, and for three days he did nothing but think. Then he reached a decision. "I will send my grandchildren abroad, each one to a different country. They must look for a husband or wife there. For all sorts of reasons, small rabbits have small children, while big rabbits have such big children that they outgrow their cribs before they can walk. The Esterhazys, being very small, should marry very big rabbits, and then their children will be just the right size."

One day, just before spring began, the old Lord dressed up in his best purple velvet suit and personally saw off each little

rabbit at the train station in Vienna. "Remember to eat well. Just carrots, salads, and nourishing local foods. No sweets!" he reminded each bunny.

The crowd of relatives roared in approval and threw bars of bittersweet chocolate.

The youngest of this clan of grandchildren was named His Lordship Michael Paul Anton Maria, Prince Esterhazy the 12,792nd of Bunnimore and Burrow-of-Austria, Earl of Snack, Count of Cucumbria, Cabbage Head and Leekfielt, Commander of Welshrabbits.

But, of course, no rabbit in his right mind called His Lordship by his full name. Actually, all rabbits have very long names, but they only go by their last names. Remember that! From now on, we will refer to our hero simply as Esterhazy.

And since Esterhazy was the very youngest in the entire family, he was the very last to leave home. Lord Esterhazy had decided that his grandson should try his luck in Berlin, a rather odd city, because one half of it belonged to one country, called East Germany, and the other half to another country called West Germany—an arrangement a little bit like Kansas City, one part of which belongs to the state of Kansas, the other to the state of Missouri. East and West Germany were not friendly neighbors, though, the way Kansas and Missouri are, and for quite a long time now, they had kept their city halves separated by a huge wall.

The night before he left, Lord Esterhazy took our hero aside and gave him some advice. "Now's your chance, my dear boy. If you want your children to be nice, big bunnies, then you'll have to get married to a nice, big bunny," he said. "And I have one hint for you: For all sorts of reasons, a wall runs right through the middle of the city. And the rabbits of Berlin all live behind that wall."

Esterhazy kissed His Lordship's paw gratefully and boarded the train going to the city of Berlin.

As the train pulled out of the station, Esterhazy settled back confidently into the cushions. He looked out at his parents and countless relatives all weeping and felt curiously

thrilled. He was sure he would have no trouble finding a wife in Berlin and living there happily ever after.

He arrived with a smile on his face.

The train station in Berlin was small and dim and very cold. Strange-looking people stood around and eyed him with hostility, or, worse, hungry expressions. He slunk along the lockers, looking for the exit. He went down some stairs. He went up some stairs. He couldn't seem to find the way out.

Finally, a dog approached him. He was the strong, ugly type Esterhazy hated most. The dog said in a rough voice, "This station is not for bunny rabbits. If you don't scram, I'll turn you into a meatball." Then he jerked his nose in the direction of four swinging doors that Esterhazy had not noticed before. They led to the street.

Esterhazy found himself on one of Berlin's main streets. Esterhazy hated shopping, so he ignored the bright lights and the big stores. He kept his ears and his nose tuned for the sound or scent of another rab-

bit. Like all Esterhazys and all rabbits, he was so nearsighted that, standing on one curb and peering with all his might across the street, he could not see the other curb.

At home, magnifying glasses lay everywhere, in all the corners, even in the broom closets and bathrooms. Old Lord Esterhazy had ordered extra thick monocles made for himself and all of his relations. In a last-ditch effort to see well, he had tried spectacles, but the doctor had said, "In your case, your Lordship, nothing will help."

For all sorts of reasons, princes, earls and knights like to be called "your lordship," or, if they are in a hurry, "sir." Remember this the next time you meet a prince! But at the moment, Lord Esterhazy didn't really care what he was called, because the eye doctor added, "And your grandson, he's even worse. Quite hopeless, sir."

Ever since, our hero had dispensed with glasses altogether and simply learned to rely on his nose. So he was quite content to hop along next to the curb, sniffing and listening. In this way he discovered that the

city had a great many dogs, hot dog stands, buses and police officers—but no rabbits.

Esterhazy had arrived in the morning, and now it was noon. He was tired and hungry. He remembered his grandfather's advice and looked for a wall. In fact, there were walls everywhere, on all sides, in front and in back of him. But no rabbits lived behind these walls, just people.

Finally, Esterhazy saw a huge shop window with a yellow sign reading, "The Easter Bunny is coming!" (Actually, it said, *"Der Osterhase kommt!"* because *Osterhase* means Easter Bunny in German. Remember to use this very important German word the next time you meet a German or an Austrian.)

And beneath the sign, perched on a little throne covered with a green wool blanket, sat a pretty brown and white rabbit with a pink ribbon around her pretty neck.

Osterhase must be a Berlin version of Esterhazy, the Austrian bunny happily concluded. He headed for the entrance.

The owner gave him a warm welcome.

"You have a beautiful rabbit in the window," said Esterhazy, hopping up on the counter. "May I have a word with her?"

"She's our last," said the shopkeeper. "No one wants a spotted Easter bunny with dark eyes. And look how big she is! But you, mister, look like the real McCoy—nice and small. My customers prefer the small ones."

"I'm an Austrian *Osterhase*," Esterhazy said proudly.

"So you're rare!" exclaimed the owner. He held open the cage door and allowed his visitor to hop inside.

"May I come in? Esterhazy's the name, pleased to meet you," he said.

"My name is Bonny," said the rabbit, looking at him curiously with her big dark eyes. She was several heads taller than he was, although she was several months younger.

"I come from Vienna," said Esterhazy. "May I ask where you're from?"

"Oh dear," replied Bonny. "I come from a lovely swampy field outside town where I was so happy!"

"If you were so happy, why did you move into the city?"

"He snatched me and brought me here," she said, pointing to the shopkeeper. "He's already sold my brothers and sisters."

Esterhazy was angry. "I will tell him to let you go at once!" he said and turned to the cage door, intent on having a stern word with the shopkeeper. But he found, to his horror, that the door was locked.

Esterhazy had been a fool. Nevertheless, he decided to make the best of his dilemma. Bonny was with him, he said to himself, and at least this way he had all the time in the world –so he thought!–to get to know her, and maybe even ask for her foot in marriage.

Esterhazy was so busy dreaming about his future with Bonny that he didn't even notice when the shopkeeper hung a sign over their cage that read, *Special on Rabbits!*

And he hardly paid attention when a small man with a big black mustache peered at him through the windowpane. The man entered the store, and before you could say "Jackrabbit," the shopkeeper had grabbed Esterhazy by the scruff of his neck and dragged him from the cage, leaving Bonny behind, looking out with big sad eyes.

He found himself in a dark, small box that jiggled.

He was just beginning to recover from his surprise when he heard a shriek, the box opened, and the man with the mustache cried, "Happy birthday, Eva!" Esterhazy was hauled out of the box again and set down in a circle of noisy children. The children danced around Esterhazy and clapped their hands.

One girl with big round glasses refused to join in. She looked at Esterhazy and said, "Frankly, Daddy, a rabbit coat would have been better. Or a motorcycle." The man she

called Daddy sighed. "Coats don't smell," said Eva. "He'll have to have a bath."

She picked Esterhazy up by the ears and dragged him off into a white room. The other children ran behind her, and Esterhazy felt himself sinking into a hot broth. He made a terrible fuss, kicking and thrashing. You must always remember: Rabbits are afraid of water, and they cannot stand to be bathed.

The man called Daddy rescued Esterhazy from drowning. But his daughter had a tantrum. "He's *my* rabbit!" she hollered.

"I thought you preferred a rabbit coat. Or a motorcycle."

The children laughed, and Eva threw a bigger tantrum. Daddy wrapped Esterhazy in a big towel and carefully carried him out of the bathroom.

"Here's your new home," he said and placed him in a wooden box.

Imagine, his new home was furnished with nothing but old newspapers.

Soon Esterhazy settled into a dull routine of eating, sleeping and letting Eva's horrible friends handle him. He grew so bored that he began to read the newspapers on the floor of his box. To his surprise, there was never any news about rabbits. Only about people! Once he found a long story about a wall running through the city. But in the pictures Esterhazy could not find any rabbits at all, and the man who had written the story even claimed that the wall was bad and should be removed.

Esterhazy shook his head and turned the pages until he reached the advertisements. He found lovely chocolates there, but, unfortunately, he knew he couldn't eat pictures of chocolates.

It was a humdrum life. Sometimes Eva brought him carrots and lettuce. Sometimes she let him out of the box. But then she felt it necessary to hand out a million rules about how to behave outside the box:

"Esterhazy, we do not make you-know-what on my pillow!"

"Esterhazy! We do not keep carrots in my bed!"

"Esterhazy, what has gotten into you!"

Eva's father was also always doing something wrong.

Once Esterhazy saw Daddy try on a new pair of boxer shorts. They were the nicest boxer shorts in the world, with a black and yellow leopardskin pattern. Daddy looked really wild in them. Esterhazy longed to try on those boxer shorts.

One day he did. He stood way up on his hind legs to look at himself in the mirror.

"Esterhazy! How dare you!"

Eva told him to put them right back.

One day she came home from school with a big paper bag.

"What do you have in there?" asked Esterhazy.

"Easter bunnies," replied Eva.

They were tiny chocolate rabbits wrapped in silver paper.

"On Easter Sunday, I'll eat them up, all of them!" said Eva.

"How about saving one for me?"

"Bunny rabbits don't eat Easter bunnies," she said carelessly.

When she had gone to bed, Esterhazy said to himself, "Let's see if bunny rabbits don't eat Easter bunnies!"

And he ate up all of her chocolate bunny rabbits, leaving only the silver wrappings. He was so full, he could hardly move. And he was terrified of what Eva would do.

The next morning, he waited for Daddy to go to work. When Daddy opened the door, Esterhazy ran out between his legs and zigzagged away. No more Evas, please, he thought.

Since Esterhazy had been reading the newspapers, he knew that at Eastertime rabbits could easily find jobs. So upon reaching the freedom of the street, he ran to the nearest department store and applied for work as an Easter Bunny. The boss wanted some proof that Esterhazy could handle the job. Esterhazy told him, "Sir, I *am* an Easter Bunny. I am an Esterhazy, the Austrian version."

The man said, "You're hired, sir. An honor." And he showed Esterhazy to his new workplace in the shop window.

Esterhazy found the work highly amusing. All he had to do was sit there and watch people stare at him. He was allowed to stare back. He found that he could amuse himself and his audience by thumping with his hind legs, or tearing into a lettuce leaf, or turning somersaults, or playing dead. "How cute!" the audience exclaimed.

On the Saturday before Easter, the sidewalk in front of his window was so crowded with shoppers that he thought of asking the boss for a raise.

But the following Monday, the boss called Esterhazy to his office. "Okay, you old chimpanzee, Easter's over. Get out." And he tossed Esterhazy outside.

He was miserable. Motorcycles and buses roared past. (You should know that rabbits

have sensitive ears, which are so large that they can't possibly hold them shut. Besides, they need their front paws for walking.) And furthermore, it had been raining all day and it was wet outdoors (rabbits, remember, are afraid of water). There was nothing to eat, either, aside from chewed-up chewing gum, beer cans and sausage ends. And when he scooted past the pet shop and couldn't see Bonny anywhere, he became even more discouraged.

After a while, Esterhazy sought refuge under a red van. At least it was dry under there. Soon he noticed a pleasant smell. He sniffed and decided the vehicle smelled like cake and apple pie.

He looked around carefully and saw that the door of the van was open. He jumped in. The front of the van looked normal, but the back was lined with layer cakes still in their pans. Under one of the cake pans, Esterhazy found a perfect burrow, filled with blankets and old newspapers. He nibbled cake crumbs, curled up, and soon fell asleep.

When he woke up, it was dark out-

side, and the red van was parked in front of a bakery. Esterhazy found a flashlight under the blanket and wrote a long letter to the old Lord, his grandfather:

"As far as I can tell, there is only one other rabbit in all of Berlin. Her name is Bonny, and she is very pretty and very big. But she has disappeared, and I cannot find her anywhere. Nor can I find the wall that you told me about, although I have seen it in the newspapers. It is hard to find a steady job here. I worked as an Easter Bunny in a department store, and although I was really good at it, they kicked me out. Right now I am living in a van. I can't complain. I haven't forgotten your advice, but there are no vegetables to be found in my new home, only divine cakes with all kinds and colors of fillings and toppings, so I am being forced against my will to live off sweets."

The driver of the van had curly hair and a nice singing voice. He was always in a good mood. Fortunately, he was so messy that he never tidied up his van. Nor did he count the cakes in the back, so he never noticed that someone was living and eating there.

When the man opened the back door of his van to remove or load the cakes, Esterhazy tucked his ears down and stayed as quiet as a mouse. As the man drove through the city, delivering cakes to shops and restaurants, Esterhazy peered through the window and looked for the wall. He saw no sign of it.

Weeks passed. Summer came.

One sunny Sunday morning, Esterhazy woke up when a woman said, "Robert! Robert! Let's take a trip somewhere."

So the man's name was Robert, and the short chubby woman waving her handbag at

Robert was probably his wife.

"This van is a pigsty," she declared, but in a friendly way, as if she liked pigs. "Let me clean up first. Get me a broom, Max," she ordered the little boy hanging around her skirts.

Then she opened the door and started removing cake pans. "What's this?" she cried.

Esterhazy had been found out.

"Pleased to meet you. Esterhazy's my name."

"*Wie suess!*" cried Robert, which means "how sweet" in German, and began petting him. Max was delighted.

They drove to a field. At last, Esterhazy could go through his paces. He ran like greased lightning. He was the only rabbit around, and everyone admired him.

From then on, they treated Esterhazy as part of the family. Max played card games with him and Robert drove all over the city with him. He could eat as much apple pie as he wanted, and at night he read the newspapers until he fell asleep on the living room sofa.

One day Robert said to his wife, whose name was Henrietta, "Let's go out for dinner."

"Not without Esterhazy," pleaded Max.

"You can't take rabbits to restaurants," fretted Henrietta.

"But why not?" asked Robert.

They went to a wonderful restaurant that served the freshest greens and all kinds of other vegetables. You may find this hard to believe, but Esterhazy was finally sick of layer cake and apple pie. He ordered a large mixed salad.

The waiter was an evil-looking giant. "I can recommend the special of the day—roast rabbit," he said.

Esterhazy's ears began to twitch.

"You don't mean they eat rabbits here," he said fearfully.

"Very tender today," replied the waiter, "with a crispy crust."

Esterhazy hoped this was only a tasteless joke. But what if it wasn't? Before he even got his meal, he might be turned into one. Some risks are worth taking. Others are not. He hopped up from his chair and beat it back to the van. His evening was ruined. He wrote to old Lord Esterhazy:

> *"I have learned that there are Rabbit-Eaters in Berlin. And still*
> *no sign of my friend Bonny."*

It was maddening. While the newspapers reported constantly about a wall, which they referred to as The Wall, Esterhazy never caught a glimpse of it. Finally he plucked up his courage and asked his friend, "Robert, tell me the truth. Is there really such a thing as The Wall?"

Robert laughed. "Sure there is. Would you like to see it?"

"Would I ever!" said Esterhazy.

That Sunday, the entire family drove for miles through the city. The air smelled of soggy leaves and chestnuts. It was autumn, Esterhazy knew. He was so excited that he didn't dare look out the window. "Max, you tell me when we're there," he said and crawled into his old burrow beneath the cake tins. He pulled some newspapers and rags over his head. The van stopped abruptly.

A voice said, "Passports please!"

And then another voice asked, "What are you carrying in there?"

"Nothing, really," replied Robert.

"What's all that in the back there?" persisted the voice suspiciously.

"Some layer cakes, apple pie, wrappers, rags, what have you."

"We forgot to clean up," said Henrietta.

"Well, then," said the voice. "Let's have a look."

And a giant hand began to root in the very pile of papers where Esterhazy was hiding. He was terrified. With a huge leap, he went through the window and took off like a shot.

"Stop!" cried the voice. It belonged to a man wearing a green uniform, carrying a gun, who looked like he ate rabbits for breakfast.

"Esterhazy, where are you?" cried Robert.

"Come back!" cried Henrietta.

"Please!" cried Max.

But Esterhazy was already way out of earshot, hopping as fast as he could go. Soon he saw a wall, and there was no doubt that it was The Wall. It was an endlessly high, endlessly long, endlessly dreary gray wall, and it seemed to take forever to hop to the edge of it. The field behind it smelled wonderful, though. It smelled of rabbits.

"Tallyho!" called a rabbit's voice. "Do we know you?"

The field was full of rabbits, and they gave Esterhazy a merry welcome. When the other rabbits realized that he was a real Esterhazy, they were quite proud. "A gentleman," they said. "Come on, we'll show you our burrow."

At the far end of the burrow, Esterhazy saw a very beautiful brown and white spotted rabbit. He was shocked because she was so big.

"Esterhazy! My dearest Esterhazy!" she cried.

"Bonny!" he cried back and kissed her. He had to stand way up on his tiptoes to reach her, because she was almost twice as tall as he. And she smelled delightful.

Bonny showed him all the corners of the burrow and invited him into her own little apartment in the back. She told him about how the shopkeeper had shooed her into the street the day after Easter. She told him about their lives behind The Wall, how they had soldiers there to guard them against dogs, cars, and Rabbit-Eaters. The soldiers threw them leftover sandwiches, sometimes a piece of ham or cake. It wasn't gourmet cooking, but a bunny could get used to it. And this was certainly the most peaceful place in the whole world.

In a postcard to the old Lord Esterhazy, he wrote:

> *"Tallyho from the Berlin Wall. Love from your grandson and*
> *his friend Bonny.*
> *P.S. We're fine, even though we live off of leftovers."*

And so the two lived happily ever after in the burrow behind The Wall. Until . . .

Until one night, when a dreadful noise began. Hundreds of people began tramping around on the rabbits' field, all yelling loudly to tear down The Wall. Many carried hammers and drills, and they busied themselves destroying The Wall.

"Why are they doing this?" asked Esterhazy.

"This Wall must come down!" the people cried. "East and West Germany will no longer be divided by walls guarded by armed soldiers."

The next day the field had been trampled black and brown by people's shoes and boots, and Esterhazy couldn't even see the grass. The Wall was gone, except for a few fragments. The people were overjoyed, but Esterhazy and Bonny couldn't quite share their enthusiasm.

"Berlin is not the same without a Wall," said Bonny. "For people, it's better, but for rabbits, it's worse. It's become rather uncomfortable for us rabbits now, wouldn't you say?"

"I have an idea," said Esterhazy. "Let's move to the country."

It was decided. They hopped along together. When they had passed the last houses of the city, they sat down to rest and nibble on grass.

"I know I'm rather short," said Esterhazy. "But perhaps you'll marry me anyway."

"I'd love to," said Bonny.

You should know that it takes exactly six weeks, and not one minute longer, for rabbits to have babies. Six weeks after this conversation, letters were sent out to Esterhazys all over the world. They read:

HIS LORDSHIP MICHAEL PAUL ANTON MARIA, PRINCE ESTERHAZY

the 12,792nd of Bunnimore and Burrow-of-Austria, Earl of Snack, Count of Cucumbria,

Cabbage Head and Leekfielt, Commander of Welshrabbits, and his wife

BONNY HELEN THERESA EMALIA

of Muddy-Meadows in the Boondocks have the pleasure of announcing the births of:

JOHN NAPOLEON MORRIS KASIMIR MICHAEL ESTERHAZY

the 12,793rd,

FRANK MARK NICHOLAS ALEXANDER MICHAEL ESTERHAZY

the 12,794th,

PHILIP JOSEPH VALENTINE JULIUS MICHAEL ESTERHAZY

the 12,795th,

MARIA AMELIA CAROLINE MIMI AUGUST ESTERHAZY

the 12,796th,

EMILIA JOANNA ELIZABETH MIMI GABRIELA ESTERHAZY

the 12,797th, and

THERESA LEOPOLD MIMI JOSEPHINE ESTERHAZY

the 12,798th.

From that moment on, the Esterhazys really did live happily ever after. Today, the fields and meadows outside of Berlin are full of cheerful, medium-sized bunnies, and if you listen to them speaking, you will notice that they all have a slight Austrian accent.

Published in 1994 by Creative Editions
123 South Broad Street
Mankato, Minnesota 56001

Creative Editions is an imprint of The Creative Company.
This title is published as a joint venture between The Creative
Company and American Education Publishing.

Art Director: Rita Marshall
Design: Stephanie Blumenthal

Library of Congress Cataloging-in-Publication Data
Dische, Irene.
[Esterhazy. English]
Esterhazy / written by Irene Dische and Hans Magnus
Enzensberger : illustrated by Michael Sowa.
Translated from the German with the same title.
Summary: Chronicles the adventures of Prince Esterhazy, a
rabbit who goes to Berlin to find a bride and witnesses the
destruction of the Berlin Wall.
ISBN 1-56846-091-0
[1. Rabbits—Fiction.   2. Berlin Wall, Berlin, Germany,
1961–1989—Fiction.]   I. Enzensberger, Hans
Magnus.   II. Sowa, Michael, 1945–   ill.   III. Title.
PZ7.D6227Es   1994
[Fic]—dc20   94-4658   CIP   AC